Anonymous

Mother Goose's Melodies

Containing all that Have Ever Come to Light of her Memorable Writings

Anonymous

Mother Goose's Melodies
Containing all that Have Ever Come to Light of her Memorable Writings

ISBN/EAN: 9783337094188

Printed in Europe, USA, Canada, Australia, Japan

Cover: Foto ©Andreas Hilbeck / pixelio.de

More available books at **www.hansebooks.com**

THERE WAS AN OLD WOMAN, SHE LIVED IN A SHOE.

MOTHER GOOSE'S
Melodies.

CONTAINING ALL THAT HAVE EVER COME TO LIGHT

—OF—

Her Memorable Writings.

Illustrated throughout
WITH ENGRAVINGS.

PUBLISHED BY JAMES MILLER,
647 BROADWAY.

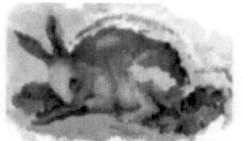

MOTHER GOOSE'S MELODIES.

CONTAINING

ALL THAT HAVE EVER COME TO LIGHT

—OF—

Her Memorable Writings.

WITHOUT ABRIDGEMENT,

ILLUSTRATED THROUGHOUT WITH ENGRAVINGS.

NEW YORK:
PUBLISHED BY JAMES MILLER,
(SUCCESSOR TO C. S. FRANCIS & CO.,)
647 BROADWAY.

MOTHER GOOSE'S MELODIES.

PAT-A-CAKE, pat-a-cake, baker's man;
   So I will, master, as fast as I can:
Pat it, and pick it, and mark it with B,
Put it in the oven for Baby and me.

WHEN I was a little boy, I washed my
      mammy's dishes,
Now I am a great boy I roll in golden riches.

FOR every evil under the sun,
    There is a remedy, or there is none.
If there be one, try and find it ;
If there be none, never mind it.

IF a man who turnips cries,
    Cries not when his father dies,
It is a proof that he would rather
Have a turnip than his father.

PEAS-PUDDING hot, peas-pudding cold,
    Peas-pudding in the pot nine days old.
Some like it hot, some like it cold,
Some like it in the pot, nine days old.

AS I was going along, long, long,
    A singing a comical song, song, song,
The lane that I went was so long, long, long,
And the song that I sung was so long, long,
        long,
And so I went singing along.

ROUND about, round about, gooseberry-
        pie,
My father loves good ale, and so do I.

TELL-TALE, tit! your tongue shall be slit,
    And all the dogs in the town shall have
        a little bit !

WILLIE boy, Willie boy,
    Where are you going?
    O let us go with you,
    This sunshiny day.

I'm going to the
    meadow,
To see them a
    mowing,
I'm going to help
    the girls
Turn the new hay.

THERE was a little man,
    And he had a little gun,
And his bullets were made of lead,
He shot John Sprig
Through the middle of his wig,
And knocked it right off his head.

VINEGAR, veal, and venison,
    Are very good victuals I vow.

JACK and Jill went up the hill,
    To fetch a pail of water;
Jack fell down, and broke his crown.
    And Jill came tumbling a'ter.

———

PUSSY sits behind the log, how can she be fair?
Then comes in the little dog, pussy, are you there?
So, so, dear mistress Pussy, pray tell me how you do?
I thank you, little dog, I'm very well just now.

———

THE little black dog ran round the house,
    And set the bull a roaring.
And drove the monkey in the boat,
    Who set the oars a rowing,
And scared the cock upon the rock,
    Who crack'd his throat with crowing.

BOYS and girls come out to play,
   The moon does shine as bright as day,
Leave your supper, and leave your sleep,
And meet your playfellows in the street.
Come with a whoop, and come with a call,
And come with a good will, or not at all.
   Up the ladder and down the wall,
   A halfpenny loaf will serve us all.
You find milk and I'll find flour,
And we'll have a pudding in half an hour.

DAFFY-DOWN-DILLY has come up to
   town,
In a green petticoat and a bright yellow
   gown,
And her little blue eyes are peeping around.

THREE children sliding on the ice,
　Upon a summer's day;
It so fell out, they all fell in,
　The rest they ran away.

Now had these children been at home,
　Or sliding on dry ground,
Ten thousand pounds to one penny,
　They had not all been drown'd.

You parents that have children dear,
　And eke you that have none,
If you would have them safe abroad,
　Pray keep them safe at home.

———

CHARLEY loves good cake and ale,
　Charley loves good candy,
Charley loves to kiss the girls,
　When they are clean and handy.

CROSS patch,
Draw the latch,
Sit by the fire and spin;
Take a cup,
And drink it up,
Then call your neighbors in.

IN fir tar is,
In oak none is.
In mud eel is,
In clay none is,
Goat eat ivy,
Mare eat oats.

WHAT care I how black I be,
Twenty pounds will marry me;
If twenty won't, forty shall,
I am my mother's bouncing girl

THE man in the moon came down too soon
To inquire the way to Norridge;
The man in the south, he burnt his mouth
With eating cold plum-porridge.

When I was a bachelor, I lived by myself,
And all the bread and cheese I got I put upon the shelf
But the rats and the mice they made such a strife,
I was forced to go to London to get myself a wife :
The roads were so bad, and the lanes were so narrow,
I was forced to take my wife home in a wheelbarrow.
The wheelbarrow broke, and my wife had a fall,
Down came the wheelbarrow, my wife and all.

———

LITTLE Jack Horner
Sat in a corner,
Eating a Christmas pie ;
He put in his thumb
And pull'd out a plum,
And said, "What a brave boy am I !"

A MAN went hunting at Reigate,
And wished to jump over a high gate;
Says the owner, "Go round,
With your horse and your hound,
For you never shall leap over my gate."

HEY my kitten, my kitten,
  And hey my kitten my
    deary,
Such a sweet pet as this
  Was neither far nor neary.

Here we go up, up, up,
  And here we go down, down,
    downy,
Here we go backward and for-
    ward,
  And here we go round,
    round, roundy.

Where was a jewel and pretty,
  Where was a sugar and
    spicy?
Hush a bye baby in the cradle,
  And we'll go abroad in a tricy.

Did his papa torment it?
  And vex his own baby will he?
Give me a hand and I'll beat him,
  With your red coral and whistle.

Here we go up, up, up,
  And here we go down, down, downy,
And here we go backward and forward,
  And here we go round, round, roundy.

TO market, to market, to buy a fat pig,
  Home again, home again, jiggety jig.
To market, to market, to buy a fat hog,
Home again, home again, jiggety jog.

IF you are to be a gentleman, as I suppose
      you to be,
You'll neither laugh nor smile for a tickling
      of the knee.

RIGADOON, rigadoon, now let him fly,
  Sit upon mother's foot, jump him up
      high.

THERE was an old woman of Leeds,
Who spent all her time in good deeds;
   She worked for the poor,
   Till her fingers were sore,
This pious old woman of Leeds!

MISS one, two, and three could never agree,
While they gossiped round a tea-caddy.

   A DUCK and a drake,
   A nice barley cake,
With a penny to pay the old baker;
   A hop and a scotch,
   Is another notch,
Slitherum, slatherum, take her.

HUSH-A-BYE, baby, upon the tree-top,
When the wind blows, the cradle will rock:
When the bough breaks the cradle will fall,
Down tumble cradle and baby and all.

UP she goes and down she comes,
If you haven't got apples, I'll give you some
   plums.

THERE was a cobbler clowting shoon,
When they were mended, they were done.

There was a monkey climbed up a tree,
When he fell down, then down fell he.

There was a butcher cut his thumb,
When it did bleed, then blood did come.

There was a navy went into Spain,
When it return'd, it came again.

THERE was an old woman lived under the
          hill,
And if she's not gone she lives there still.
Baked apples she sold, and cranberry pies,
And she's the old woman that never told lies.

WASH me and comb me,
          And lay me down softly,
And set me on a bank to dry,
     That I may look pretty,
When some one comes by.

MATTHEW, Mark, Luke, and John,
          Guard the bed that I lay on!
Four corners to my bed,
Four angels round my head;
One to watch, one to pray,
And two to bear my soul away!

WHEN the wind is in the east,
          'Tis neither good for man nor beast:
When the wind is in the north,
The skillful fisher goes not forth;
When the wind is in the south,
It blows the bait in the fishes' mouth;
When the wind is in the west,
Then 'tis at the very best.

"COME, let's to bed," says Sleepy-head;
  "Tarry a while," says Slow;
"Put on the pot," says Greedy-gut,
  "We'll sup before we go."

OH, dear, what can the matter be!
  Two old women got up in an apple-tree;
    One came down,
And the other staid up till Saturday.

SEE-SAW, Margery-daw,
  Harry shall have a new master;
He shall have but a penny a day,
Because he won't work any faster.

BONNY lass! bonny
        lass!
    Will you be mine?
You shall neither wash
        dishes
    Nor serve the wine,
But sit on a cushion
    And sew up a seam,
And you shall have straw-
        berries,
    Sugar, and cream

CRIPPLE Dick upon a stick,
    And Sandy on a sow,
Riding away to Galloway,
    To buy a pound o' woo.

THE little priest of Felton,
The little priest of Felton,
He kill'd a mouse within his house,
And ne'er a one to help him.

Mary had a pretty bird,
　　Feathers bright and yellow,
Slender legs, upon my word
　　He was a pretty fellow.
The sweetest notes he always sung,
　　Which much delighted Mary
And often where the cage was hung,
　　She stood to hear Canary.

SNAIL! snail! come out of your hole,
    Or else I'll beat you as black as a coal.
Snail! snail! put in your head,
Or else I'll beat you till you're dead.

MISTRESS MARY, quite contrary,
    How does your garden grow?
With silver bells and cockle shells,
And cowslips all a row.

HOP away, skip away, my baby wants to
    play.
My baby wants to play every day.

[*A Song set to fingers or toes.*]

1. THIS pig went to market;

2. This pig staid at home;

3. This pig had plenty to eat,

4. But this pig had none;

5. And this little pig said, "Wee, wee, wee!" All the way home.

CHARLEY WAG,
    Ate the pudding and left the bag.

HUSH-A-BYE, baby, daddy is near,
    Mammy's a lady, and that's very clear

ONCE I saw a little bird come hop, hop, hop;
So l cried, little bird, will you stop, stop, stop?
And was going to the window to say how do you do?
But he shook his little tail, and far away he flew.

A DONKEY walks
on four legs,
And I walk on two;
The last donkey I
saw
Was very like you,

BOW, wow, wow, whose dog are thou?
Little Tom Tinker's dog, bow, wow, wow.

BLOW, wind, blow! and go, mill, go!
That the miller may grind his corn;
That the baker may take it,
And into rolls make it,
And send us some hot in the morn.

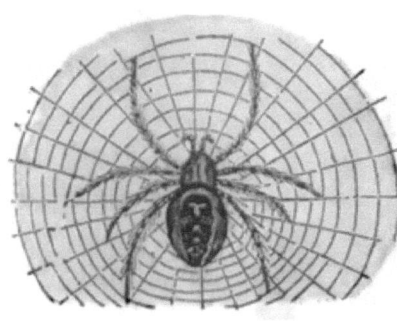

JENNY, good spinner,
Come down to your dinner,
And taste the leg of a
frog;
Then all you good people,
Look over the sseeple,
And see the cat play with
the dog.

TOM, Tom, the piper's son,
Stole a pig and away he run.
The pig was eat, and Tom was beat,
And Tom ran crying down the street.

Oh, madam, I will give you the keys of my chest,
To count my gold and silver when I am gone to rest,
If you will but walk abroad with me,
If you will but talk with me.

Oh, sir, I will accept of the keys of your chest,
To count your gold and silver when you are gone to rest,
And I will walk abroad with thee,
And I will talk with thee!

ONE a penny, two a penny, hot cross-buns;
If your daughters do not like them, give them to your
        sons.
But if you should have none of these pretty little elves,
You cannot do better than to eat them yourselves.

PUSSY-CAT eat the dumplings, the dumplings
Pussy-cat eat the dumplings.
    Mamma stood by,
     And cried, Oh, fie!
Why did you eat the dumplings?

———

TO make your candles last
for aye,
You wives and maids give
ear-o!
To put 'em out's the only
way,
Says honest John Boldero.

SWING swong, the days are long;
Up hill and down dale; butter is made in every vale;
And if that Nancy Cook is a good girl,
She shall have a spouse, and make butter anon,
Before her old grandmother grows a young man.

AS I was going by Charing Cross,
I saw a black man upon a black horse;
They told me it was King Charles the First;
Oh dear! my heart was ready to burst!

THIS is the way
the ladies ride;
Tri, tre, tre, tree,
Tri, tre, tre, tree.
This is the way the
ladies ride,
Tri, tre, tre, tree,
tri-tre-tre-tree!

This is the way the
gentlemen ride;
Gallop-a-trot,
Gallop-a-trot!
This is the way the
gentlemen ride;
Gallop- a-gallop-a
trot!

This is the way the
farmers ride;
Hobbledy-hoy,
Hobbledy-hoy!
This is the way the
farmers ride,
Hobbledy, hobble-
dy-hoy!

ONE misty, moisty morning,
  When cloudy was the weather,
I chanced to meet an old man clothed all in leather.
He began to compliment, and I began to grin,
  How do you do, and how do you do?
  And how do you do again?

FATHER SHORT came down the lane,
  Oh! I'm obliged to hammer and smite
  From four in the morning till eight at night,
For a bad master and a worse dame.

A PIE sat on a pear
tree,
A pie sat on a pear
tree,
A pie sat on a pear
tree,
Heigh O! heigh O!
heigh O!
Once so merrily
hopp'd she,
Twice so merrily
hopp'd she,
Thrice so merrily
hopp'd she,
Heigh O! heigh O!
heigh O!

I HAVE a little sister, they call her Peep, Peep,
She wades in the water, deep; deep, deep,
She climbs up the mountains, high, high, high;
My poor little sister—she has but one eye!

THE king of France, with twenty thousand men,
March'd up the hill, and then—march'd back again.

I HAD a little pony,
    His name was Dapple Gray,
I lent him to a lady,
    To ride a mile away.

She whipp'd him, she lash'd him,
    She rode him through the mire;
I would not lend my pony now
    · For all the lady's hire.

SEE a pin and pick it up.
All the day you'll have good luck;
See a pin and let it lay,
Bad luck you'll have all the day!

BARNABY BRIGHT he was a sharp cur,
He always would bark if a mouse did but stir;
But now he's grown old, and can no longer bark,
He's condemn'd by the parson to be hang'd by the clerk.

THE man in the wilderness asked me
How many strawberries grew in the sea?
I answered him as I thought good,
As many as red herrings grew in the wood.

THERE was a fat man of Bombay,
  Who was smoking one sunshiny day,
When a bird, called a snipe,
Flew away with his pipe,
Which vexed the fat man of Bombay.

THIRTY days hath September,
  April, June, and November;
February has twenty-eight alone,
And the rest have thirty-one,
Excepting leap-year, that's the time,
When February's days are twenty-nine.

BELL horses, bell horses,
  What time of day?
One o'clock, two o'clock,
  Off and away.

BAT, bat, come under my hat,
    And I will give you a slice of bacon,
And when I bake, I'll give you a cake,
    If I am not mistaken.

PUSSY-CAT, pussy-cat, where have you
      been?
I've been to London to see the Queen.
Pussy-cat, pussy-cat, what did you there?
    I frightened a little mouse under the chair.

JACK SPRAT could eat no fat,
    His wife could eat no lean;
And so, betwixt them both, you see,
    They lick'd the platter clean.

SMILING girls, rosy boys,
    Come and buy my little toys,
Monkeys made of gingerbread,
And sugar horses painted red

TO market, to market, to buy a plum-bun:
Home again, come again, market is done.

HUSH a bye, baby, on the tree top,
When the wind blows, the cradle will rock;
When the bough bends, the cradle will fall,
Down will come baby, bough, cradle, and all.

UPON my word and honor,
    As I was going to Bonner,
I met a pig without a wig,
Upon my word and honor.

SATURDAY night shall be my whole care,
    To powder my locks and curl my hair;
On Sunday morning my love will come in,
And marry me then with a pretty gold ring.

I HAD a little dog, they called him Buff,
　I sent him to the shop for a hap'orth of
　　snuff:
But he lost the bag, and spilt the snuff
So take that cuff, and that's enough.

HARK! hark! the dogs do bark,
　Beggars are coming to town,
Some in jags, and some in rags,
　And some in velvet gown.

LADY-BIRD, lady-bird,
　Fly away home,
Your house is on fire,
Your children will burn.

DANCE, little baby, dance up high,
　Never mind, baby, mother is nigh;
Crow and caper, caper and crow;
There, little baby, there you go.
Up to the ceiling, down to the ground,
Backwards and forwards, round and round;
Dance, little baby, and mother will sing,
With the merry coral, ding, ding, ding!

COLD and raw the north winds blow,
　Bleak in the morning early;
All the hills are covered with snow,
And winter's now come fairly.

PRETTY flower, tell me
    why,
  All your leaves do open
    wide
Every morning, when on
    high
  The noble sun begins to
    ride.
This is why, my lady fair,
  If you would the reason
    know,
For betimes the pleasant
    air
  Very cheerfully doth
    blow.

And the birds on every tree
  Sing a merry, merry tune,
And the busy honey-bee
  Comes to suck my sugar
    soon.

This is all the reason why
  I my little leaves undo:
Lady, lady, wake and try
  If I have not told you
    true.

Taffy was a Welshman,
  Taffy was a thief,
Taffy came to my house,
  And stole a piece of beef.
I went to Taffy's house,
  Taffy wasn't at home,
Taffy came to my house,
  And stole a marrow bone.
I went to Taffy's house,
  Taffy was in bed,
I took the marrow bone,
  And beat about his head.

The damsels are churning for curds and whey;
The damsels are churning for curds and whey;
The lads in the fields are making hay,
    With a hop, step, and a jump.

THERE was an old woman had
        nothing,
    And there came thieves to
        rob her;
When she cried out she made
        no noise,
    But all the country heard
        her,

YOU shall have an apple,
    You shall have a plum;
You shall have a rattle-basket,
    When your dad comes home.

A COW and a calf,
An ox and a half,
Forty good shillings and three,
Is not that enough tocher
For a shoemaker's daughter,
A bonny lass with a black
        e'e?

LITTLE maid, pretty maid,
   whither goest thou?
Down in the forest to milk
   my cow.
Shall I go with thee?   No,
   not now;
When I send for thee, then
   come thou.

———

LITTLE   lad, little lad,
   where wast thou born?
Far off, in Lancashire, under
   a thorn,
Where they sup sour milk in
   a ram's horn.

SOME little mice
sat in a barn
to spin.
Pussy came by,
and she popped
her head in;
"Shall I come in
and cut your
threads off?"

"Oh no, kind sir, you will snap our heads
off."

LITTLE Robin Redbreast sat upon a rail:
Niddle noddle went his head, and wag-
gle went his tail.

THERE was a piper who had a cow,
But he had no hay to give her;
So he took his pipes and played a tune,
Consider, old cow, consider!

GOOSEY, goosey, gander, whither shall I wander?
Up stairs, and down stairs, and in my lady's chamber.
There I met an old man who would not say his prayers;
I took him by the left leg, and threw him down stairs.

DIDDLE, diddle, dumpling, my son John
    Went to bed with his breeches on;
One shoe off, the other shoe on,
Diddle, diddle, dumpling, my son John.

ONCE in my life I married a wife,
    And where do you think I found her?
On Gretna Green, in velvet sheen,
    And I took up a stick to pound her.
She jumped over a barberry-bush,
    And I jumped over a timber:
I showed her a gay gold ring,
    And she showed me her finger.

THERE was a rat, for want of stairs,
    Went down a rope to say his prayers.

IF all the world was apple-pie,
    And all the sea was ink,
And all the trees were bread and cheese
    What should we have to drink?
It's enough to make an old man
    Scratch his head and think.

DINGTY, diddledy, my mammy's maid,
    She stole oranges, I am afraid.
Some in her pocket, some in her sleeve,
She stole oranges, I do believe.

DID you not hear of Betty Pringle's pig?
It was not very little nor yet very big;
The pig sat down upon a dung-hill,
And there poor piggy he made his will.

Betty Pringle came to see this pretty pig
That was not very little nor yet very big;
This little piggy it lay down and died,
And Betty Pringle sat down and cried.

Then Johnny Pringle buried this very pretty pig,
That was not very little nor yet very big.
So here's an end of the song of all three,
Johnny Pringle, Betty Pringle, and little Piggy.

THE Quaker's wife got up to bake,
  Her children all about her,
She gave them every one a cake,
  And the miller wants his moulter.

THE white dove sat on the castle wall,
   I bend my bow and shoot her I shall;
I put her in my glove, both feathers and all;
I laid my bridle upon the shelf,
If you will any more, sing it yourself.

SEE, see! what shall I see?
   A horse's head where his tail should be.

THERE were three crows sat on a stone,
       Fal la, la, la, lal, de,
Two flew away, and then there was one,
       Fal la, la, la, lal, de,
The other crow finding himself alone,
       Fal la, la, la, lal, de.
He flew away, and then there was none,
       Fal la, la, la, lal, de.

THE lion and the unicorn
   Were fighting for the crown—
The lion beat the unicorn
   All about the town.
Some gave them white bread,
   And some gave them brown,
Some gave them plum-cake,
   And sent them out of town.

THERE was an old man,
  And he had a calf;
  And that's half;
He took him out of the stall,
And tied him to the wall;
  And that's all.

———.

SNAIL! snail! come out
  of your hole,
Or else I'll beat you as black
  as a coal.

———

A LITTLE boy and a little girl
  Lived in an alley.
Said the little boy to the little girl,
  Shall I? oh, shall I?
Said the little girl to the little boy,
  What will you do?
Said the little boy to the little girl,
  I will kiss you.

Simple Simon met a pieman
   Going to the fair:
Says Simple Simon to the pieman,
   "Let me taste your ware."

Says the pieman to Simpie Simon,
   "Show me first your penny."
Says Simple Simon to the pieman,
   "Indeed I have not any."

THERE was a jolly miller
Lived on the river Dee,
He looked upon his pillow,
And there he saw a flea
Oh! Mr. Flea,
You have been biting me,
And you must die:
So he cracked his bones
Upon the stones,
And there he let him lie.

ST. DUNSTAN, as the story goes,
Once pulled the tempter by the nose,
With red-hot tongs, which made him
roar,
That he was heard ten miles or more.

LITTLE girl, little girl, where
have you been?
Gathering roses to give to the
Queen.
Little girl, little girl, what
gave she you?
She gave me a diamond as big
as my shoe.

JOHN O'Gudgeon he was a wild man,
　　He whipt his children now and then :
When he whipt them he made them dance,
Out of Ireland into France.

GOOSEY goosey gander,
　　Whither dost thou wander?
Up stairs, down stairs,
　In my lady's chamber :
There I met an old man,
　　Who would not say his prayers ;
I took him by the left leg,
　　And threw him down stairs.

UP in the green orchard there is a green
　　tree,
The finest of pippins that ever you see :
The apples are ripe, and ready to fall,
And Reuben and Robin shall gather them all.

LAZY Tom with jacket blue,
　　Stole his father's gouty shoe.
The worst of harm that dad can wish him,
Is that his gouty shoe may fit him.

THREE straws on a staff,
　　Would make a baby cry and laugh.

WHERE are you going to, my pretty maid?
  I am going a milking, sir, she said.
May I go with you, my pretty maid?
You're kindly welcome, sir, she said.

ROBIN the Bobbin the
big-bellied Ben,
He ate more meat than
fourscore men;
He ate a cow, he ate a
calf,
He ate a butcher and a
half;
He ate a church, he ate
a steeple,
He ate the priest and
all the people!

Three wise men of Gotham
Went to sea in a bowl
And if the bowl had been stronger
My song had been longer.

BOBBY SHAFTOE'S gone to sea,
Silver buckles on his knee;
He'll come back and marry me,
       Pretty Bobby Shaftoe.

Bobby Shaftoe's fat and fair,
Combing down his yellow hair,
He's my love forevermore,
       Pretty Bobby Shaftoe.

THERE was an old woman,
  She lived in a shoe,
She had so many children
  She didn't know what to
    do;
She gave them some broth
  Without any bread,
She   whipped   them   all
    soundly,
  And put them to bed.

HICKETY, pickety,
  My black hen,
She lays eggs
For gentlemen;
Gentlemen come
Every day
To see what my
Black hen doth
  lay.

HIGH diddle doubt, my candle's out,
  And my little dame's not come :
So saddle my hog, and bridle my dog,
And fetch my little dame home.

THERE was a little one-eyed gunner,
  Killed all the birds that died last sum-
    mer.

LITTLE boy blue, come blow up your horn,
   The sheep's in the meadow, the cow's in
      the corn;
Where's the little boy that looks after the
      sheep?
He's under the haycock fast asleep.

AS I was going to sell my eggs,
   I met a man with bandy legs,
Bandy legs and crooked toes,
I tripp'd up his heels, and he fell on his nose.

HOW many miles to Baby-
    lon?
Threescore miles and ten.
Can I get there by candle-
    light?
Yes, and back again.

———

MISS Jane had a bag, and a mouse was in it,
She opened the bag, he was out in a minute;
The Cat saw him jump, and run under the table,
And the dog said, catch him, puss, soon as you're able.

———

WHAT'S the news of the day,
Good neighbor, I pray?
They say the balloon
Has gone up to the moon.

———

PUSSY cat, pussy cat where have
    you been?
I've been to London to see the Queen.
Pussy cat, pussy cat, what did you
    there?
I frightened a little mouse under the
    chair.

IS John Smith with-
    in?
Yes, that he is;
Can he set a shoe?
Ay, marry, two;
Here a nail, there a
    nail,
Tick, tack, too

LITTLE King Boggen he built a fine hall,
Pie-crust, and pastry-crust, that was the wall;
The windows were made of black puddings and white,
And slated with pancakes—you ne'er saw the like.

RIDE, baby, ride,
  Pretty baby shall ride,
And have a little puppy-dog tied
    to her side,
And have little pussy-cat tied to
    the other,
And away she shall ride to see her
    grandmother;
  To see her grandmother,
  To see her grandmother, in Ger-
    mantown.

WHO comes here? A grenadier.
    What do you want? A pot of beer.
Where's your money? I forgot.
Get you gone, you drunken sot.

MY little man and I fell out;
    I'll tell you what 'twas all about:
I had money, and he had none,
And that's the way the row begun.

HOW many days has my baby to play?
    Saturday, Sunday, Monday,
Tuesday, Wednesday, Thursday, Friday,
  Saturday, Sunday, Monday.

LITTLE blue Betty lived in a den,
    She sold good ale to gentlemen:
Gentlemen came there every day,
And little blue Betty hopped away.
She hopped up stairs to make her bed,
And she tumbled down and broke her head.

BYE, oh, my baby!
    When I was a lady,
Oh, then my poor babe didn't cry!
  But my baby is weeping
  For want of good keeping.
Oh, I fear my poor baby will die.

THERE were two blackbirds
   Sitting on a hill,
The one named Jack,
   The other nam'd Jill,
     Fly away, Jack!
     Fly away Jill!
     Come again, Jack!
     Come again, Jilll!

AWA' birds, away!
Take a little, and leave a little,
And do not come again;
For if you do,
I will shoot you through,
And there is an end of you.

SING a song of sixpence,
   A bag full of rye,
Four-and-twenty blackbirds
   Baked in a pie:
When the pie was opened
   The birds began to sing;
And wasn't this a dainty dish
   To set before the king?

HE that would thrive must rise at five;
   He that hath thriven may lie till seven;
And he that by the plough would thrive,
Himself must either hold or drive.

AS I was going to sell my eggs,
   I met a man with bandy legs,
Bandy legs and crooked toes,
I tripped up his heels and he fell on his nose.

DANCE to your daddy,
  My bonny laddy,
Dance to your ninny,
  My sweet lamb;
You shall have a fishy
In a little dishy,
And a whirligiggy,
  And some nice jam.

HUMPTY DUMPTY sat on a wall,
Humpty Dumpty had a great fall,
Not all the king's horses, nor all the king's
        men,
Could set Humpty Dumpty up again.

LITTLE Tom Tucker
Sings for his supper:
What shall he eat?
White bread and butter.
How shall he cut it
Without e'er a knife?
How will he be married
Without e'er a wife?

SNAIL, snail, come put out your horn,
 To-morrow is the day to shear the corn.

SEE, see. What shall I see?
 A horse's head where his tail should be.

LITTLE boy, pretty boy, where were you
  born?
In Lincolnshire, master, come blow the cow's
  horn.

EGGS, butter, cheese, bread,
  Stick, stock, stone, dead.
Stick him up, stick him down,
Stick him in the old man's crown.

HEY ding a ding, what shall I sing?
  How many holes in a skimmer?
Four-and-twenty—my stomach's empty;
  Pray, mamma, give me some dinner.

THREE little kittens lost their mittens;
  And they began to cry,
Oh! mother, dear, we very much fear,
That we have lost our mittens.
Lost your mittens! you naughty kittens!
  Then you shall have no pie.
    Mee-ow, mee-ow, mee-ow.
  No, you shall have no pie.
    Mee-ow, mee-ow, mee-ow.

WHEN I was a little he,
  My mother took me on her knee;
Smiles and kisses gave with joy,
And called me oft her darling boy.

LITTLE Bo-peep has lost
her sheep,
And cannot tell where to find
'em ;
Leave them alone, and they'll
come home,
And bring their tails behind
'em.

Little Bo-peep fell fast asleep,
And dreamt she heard them bleating ;
When she awoke, she found it a joke,
For still they all were fleeting.

Then up she took her little crook,
Determin'd for to find them ;
She found them indeed, but
it made her heart bleed,
For they'd left their tails
behind them.

It happen'd one day, as
Bo-peep did stray
Unto a meadow hard by :
There she espied their tails
side by side,
All hung on a tree to dry.

The queen of hearts,
   She made some tarts,
All on a summer's day;
   The knave of hearts
   He stole those tarts,
And with them ran away:
   The king of hearts
   Call'd for those tarts,
And beat the knave full sore,
   The knave of hearts
   Brought back those tarts,
And said he'd ne'er steal more.

The king of spades
   He kiss'd the maids,
Which vex'd the queen full sore;
   The queen of spades
   She beat those maids
And turn'd them out of door;
   The knave of spades
   Grieved for those jades,
And did for them implore;
   The queen so gent,
   She did relent,
And vow'd she'd ne'er strike more.

The king of clubs
  He often drubs
His loving queen and wife;
  The queen of clubs
  Returns him snubs,
And all is noise and strife;
  The knave of clubs
  Gives winks and rubs,
And swears he'll take her part;
  For when our kings
  Will do such things,
They should be made to smart.

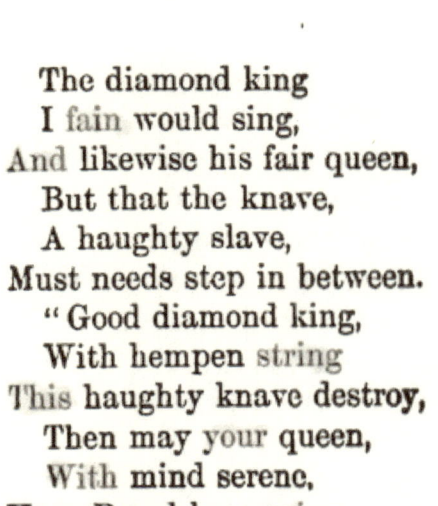

The diamond king
  I fain would sing,
And likewise his fair queen,
  But that the knave,
  A haughty slave,
Must needs step in between.
  " Good diamond king,
  With hempen string
This haughty knave destroy,
  Then may your queen,
  With mind serene,
Your Royal love enjoy

CUSHY cow, bonny, let down thy milk,
And I will give thee a gown of silk;
A gown of silk and a silver tee.
If thou wilt let down thy milk to me.

———

JACK be nimble,
    Jack be quick:
And Jack jump over
    The candle-stick.

THE north wind doth blow,
And we shall have snow,
And what will poor Robin do then?
Poor thing!

He'll sit in a barn,
And to keep himself warm,
Will hide his head under his wing.
Poor thing!

———

THE cat sat asleep by the side of the fire,
The mistress snored loud as a pig:
Jack took up his fiddle by Jenny's desire,
And struck up a bit of a jig.

A CARRION crow sat
　　upon an oak,
Fol de rol, de rol, de rol,
　　de ri do,
Watching a tailor cutting
　　out his cloak;
Sing heigh ho! the carrion
　　crow,
Fol de rol, de rol, de rol,
　　de ri do.

Wife, wife! bring me my bow,
　　Fol de rol, de rol, de rol, de ri do,
That I may shoot yon carrion crow;
　　Sing heigh ho! the carrion crow,
　　Fol de rol, de rol, de rol, de ri do.

The tailor he shot and miss'd his mark,
　　Fol de rol, de rol, de rol, de ri do;
And shot his own sow quite through the heart,
　　Sing heigh ho! the carrion crow,
　　Fol de rol, de rol. de rol, de ri do.

Wife, wife! bring me
  brandy in a spoon;
Fol de rol, de rol, de rol,
  de ri do,
For our old sow has fall'n
  down in a swoon
Sing heigh ho! the car-
  rion crow,
Fol de rol, de rol, de rol,
  de ri do.

A PRETTY little girl in a round-eared cap
I met in the streets t'other day;
    She gave me such a thump,
    That my heart it went bump;
I thought I should have fainted away!
I thought I should have fainted away!

IN a marble as white as milk,
Lined with skin as soft as silk;
Within a fountain crystal clear,
A golden apple doth appear.
No doors there are to this strong-hold,
Yet things break in and steal the gold.

THERE was a little man, and he had a little gun,
  And his bullets they were made of lead, lead, lead ,
He went unto the brook, and shot a little duck,
  And he hit her right through the head, head, head.
Then he went home unto his wife Joan,
  And bid her a good fire make, make, make;
For to roast the little duck he had shot at the brook,
  And he'd go and fetch home the drake, drake. drake

A DILLER, a dollar,
A ten o'clock scholar,
What makes you come so soon?
You used to come at ten o'clock,
But now you come at noon.

BARBER, barber, shave a pig,
How many hairs will make a wig?
Four-and-twenty; that's enough.
Give the poor barber a pinch of snuff

TOMMY kept a chandler's shop,
Richard went to buy a mop,
Tommy gave him such a knock,
That sent him out of his chandler's shop.

HERE'S A, B, C, D,
E, F, and G,
H, I, J, K,
L, M, N, O, P,
Q, R, S, T,
U, W, V,
X, Y, and Z.
And oh, dear me,
When shall I learn
My A, B, C?

AS Tommy Snooks and Bessy Brooks
Were walking out one Sunday,
Says Tommy Snooks to Bessy Brooks,
"To-morrow will be Monday."

WHO goes round my house this night?
None but bloody Tom!
Who steals all the sheep at night?
None but this poor one.

I WOULD if I could,
If I couldn't, how could I?
I couldn't without I could, could I?
Could you without you could, could ye?
Could ye, could ye?
You couldn't, without you could, could ye?

LITTLE Bo-peep has lost her sheep.
Leave them alone and they'll come
home,
And bring their tails behind 'em.

LITTLE Tommy Tucker,
    Sang for his supper;
What shall he eat?
White bread and butter.
How shall he cut it,
Without e'er a knife?
How will he marry
Without e'er a wife?

MOLLY, my sister, and I fell out,
    And what do you think it was about?
She loved coffee, and I loved tea,
And that was the reason we couldn't agree.

TO market, to market, to buy a penny bun:
    Home again, home again, market is done

JACK SPRAT would eat no fat,
  His wife would eat no lean;
Now was not this a pretty trick
  To make the platter clean?

DOGS in the garden, catch 'em Towser;
  Cows in the cornfield, run, boys, run;
Cats in the cream-pot, run, girls, run, girls;
Fire on the mountains, run, boys, run.

SHOE the horse, shoe the colt,
  Shoe the wild mare;
Here a nail, there a nail,
  Yet she goes bare.

THERE was a mad man,
  And he had a mad wife,
And they lived all in a mad lane!
They had three children all at a birth,
And they too were mad every one.
  The father was mad,
  The mother was mad,
The children all mad beside;
And upon a mad horse they all of them got,
And madly away did ride.

NEEDLES and pins, needles and pins,
  When a man marries his trouble begins

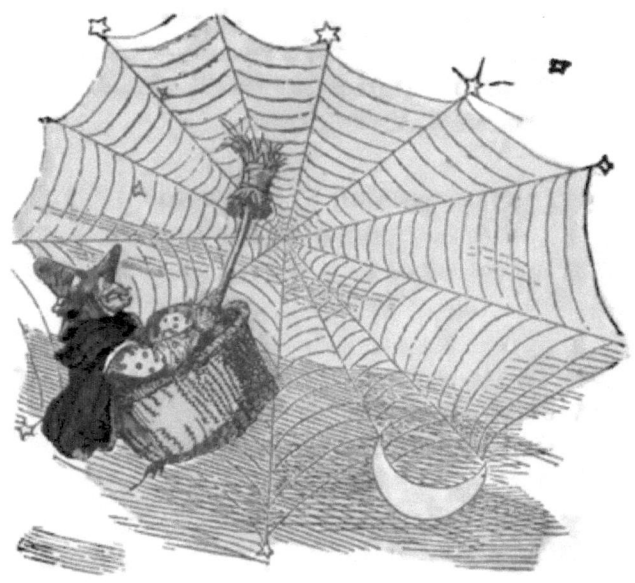

THERE was an old woman toss'd up in a
    basket,
Nineteen times as high as the moon.
Where she was going I couldn't but ask it,
For in her hand she carried a broom.

"Old woman, old woman, old woman,"
        quoth I,
"O whither, O whither, O whither, so high?"
"To brush the cobwebs off the sky!"
"Shall I go with thee?" "Aye, by and by.'

DOCTOR Foster went to Gloster
   In a shower of rain;
He stepped in a puddle up to the middle,
And never went there again.

THERE was an old woman
   Called Nothing-at-all,
Who rejoiced in a dwelling
   Exceedingly small:
A man stretched his mouth
   To its utmost extent,
And down at one gulp
   House and old woman went.

FA, Fe, Fi, Fo, Fum!
   I smell the blood of an Englishman.
Be he live or be he dead,
I'll grind his bones to make me bread.

GREEN cheese, yellow laces,
   Up and down the market-places,
Turn, cheeses, turn!

WHEN little Fred went to bed,
   He always said his prayers;
He kissed mamma, and then papa,
   And straightway went up stairs.

I CAN make diet bread,
   Thick and thin;
I can make diet bread,
   Fit for the king.

———

IF I were a little bird.
To rise upon the wing,
In the sky I would be heard,
Where larks in summer sing

Dear little birdie, soon I'd be
On every spray by side of thee;
Alas! I caunot mount so high—
And so, dear little bird good-bye

FOUR-and-twenty tailors
    Went to kill a snail,
The best man among them
    Durst not touch her tail.
She put out her horns,
    Like a little Kyloe cow :
Run, tailors, run,
    Or she'll kill you all e'en now

RUB a dub dub,
    Three men in a tub
The butcher, the baker,
The candle-stick maker ;
All jumped out of a rotten potato

THE nightingale sings when we're at rest;
The nightingale sings when we're at rest;
The little bird climbs the tree for his nest,
    With a hop, step, and a jump.

The miller he grinds his corn, his corn;
The miller he grinds his corn, his corn;
The little boy blue comes winding his horn.
    With a hop, step, and a jump.

The carter he whistles aside his team;
The carter he whistles aside his team;
And Dolly comes tripping with nice clouted cream
    With a hop, step, and a jump.

WHEN I was a little boy, my mother kept
  me in,
Now I am a great boy, and fit to serve the
 king ;
I can handle a musket, I can smoke a pipe,
I can kiss a pretty girl at ten o'clock at night.

PETER, Peter, pumpkin-eater,
  Had a wife and couldn't keep her ;
He put her in a pumpkin-shell,
And then he kept her very well.
Peter, Peter, pumpkin-eater,
Had another and didn't love her :
Peter learned to read and spell,
And then he loved her very well.

I HAD a little hen, the prettiest ever seen,
  She wash'd the dishes and kept the house clean;
She went to the mill to fetch me some flour,
She brought it home in less than an hour,
She baked me my bread, she brew'd me my ale,
She sat by the fire, and told many a fine tale.

DEAR Sensibility, O la!
I heard a little lamb cry baa!
Says I, "So you have lost mamma?"

"Baa!"

The little lamb, as I said so,
Frisking about the fields did go,
And, frisking, trod upon my toe.

"Oh!"

JOG on, jog on, the footpath way,
And merrily jump the stile, boys,
A merry heart goes all the day,
Your sad one tires in a mile, boys.

KISS me asleep, and kiss me awake,
Kiss me for dear Willie's sake.

LITTLE Jack Horner sat in the corner,
    Eating a Christmas pie:
He put in his thumb, and pull'd out a plum,
And said, "What a good boy am I!"

WE'RE all dry with drinking on't,
    We're all dry with drinking on't;
The piper kissed the fiddler's wife,
And I can't sleep for thinking on't.

THERE was a butcher cut his thumb,
    When it did bleed, blood did come.

THERE were two blind men went to see
    Two cripples run a race;
The bull did fight the humblebee,
    And scratched him in the face.

HEY diddle diddle,
    The cat and the fiddle,
The cow jumped over the moon;
    The little dog laughed
    To see such craft,
And the dish ran away with the spoon.

HICCORY, diccory, dock,
    The mouse ran up the clock;
The clock struck one,
The mouse ran down,
    Hiccory, diccory, dock.

TITE, tite, prickly pears,
    Jolly Santa Claus, what are your wares?
"A silver cup for Johnny Bowlyn—
His name engraved around the rim.
A doll for Annie, a drum for you—
I have something for every shoe."

GREAT A, little a, bouncing B!
    The cat's in the cupboard, and she can't
    see.

RIDE a cock horse to Banbury Cross,
To see a young woman jump ou a white horse,
With rings on her fingers and bells on her toes,
And she shall have music wherever she goes.

———

ROBERT BARNS, fellow fine,
Can you shoe this horse of mine,
So that I may cut a shine?
Yes good sir, and that I can,
As well as any other man;
There a nail, and here a prod,
And now, good sir, your horse is shod.

BAH, bah, black sheep, have you any wool?
Yes, marry, have I, three bags full:
One for my master, and one for my dame,
And one for the little boy who lives in the lane.

ROBIN and Richard
Were two pretty men,
They lay in bed
Till the clock struck ten;
Then up starts Robin
And looks at the sky,
Oh, brother Richard,
The sun's very high!

PETER WHITE will ne'er go right;
 Would you know the reason why?
He follows his nose where'er he goes
 And that stands all awry.

BYE, baby bumpkin,
 Where's Tony Lumpkin?
My lady's on her death-bed,
 With eating half a pumpkin.

TIDDLE liddle lightum, pitch and tar;
Tiddle liddle lightum, what's that for?

CURR dhoo, curr dhoo,
Love me, and I'll love you!

SHOE the horse, and shoe the mare;
But let the little colt go bare.

I HAD a little dog, they called him Buff,
  I sent him to the shop for a hap'orth of snuff:
But he lost the bag, and spilt the snuff,
So take that cuff, and that's enough.

CRY, baby, cry,
  Put your finger in your eye,
And tell your mother it wasn't I.

LITTLE Robin Red-breast sat upon a tree,
Up went Pussy-cat, and down went he;
Down came Pussy-cat, and away Robin ran:
Says little Robin Red-breast, "Catch me if
you can."
Little Robin Red-breast hopped upon a wall,
Pussy-cat jumped after him, and almost got
a fall.
Little Robin chirped and sang, and what did
Pussy say?
Pussy-cat said, "Mew," and Robin flew away.

COCK a doodle do,
My dame has lost her shoe;
My master's lost his fiddle-stick
And knows not what to do.

THERE was an old woman in Surrey,
Who was morn, noon, and night in a
hurry;
Call'd her husband a fool,
Drove the children to school,
The worrying old woman of Surrey.

BYE, baby bunting, father's gone a-hunting,
To get a little rabbit-skin, to wrap baby
bunting in.

IF I'd as much money as I could spend,
I never would cry old chairs to mend;
Old chairs to mend, old chairs to mend;
I never would cry old chairs to mend.

If I'd as much money as I could tell,
I never would cry old clothes to sell;
Old clothes to sell, old clothes to sell;
I never would cry old clothes to sell.

MULTIPLICATION is vexation,
   Division is as bad;
The Rule of Three doth puzzle me,
   And Practice drives me mad.

PUSSY cat, pussy cat, with a white foot,
Tomorrow is my wedding, won't you come to 'it.
I've cakes to bake, and beer to brew,
Oh! pussy cat, pussy cat, what shall I do?

———

AWAY, pretty robin, fly home to your nest,
To make you my captive I still should like best,
  And feed you with worms and with bread:
Your eyes are so sparkling, your feathers so soft,
Your little wings flutter so pretty aloft,
  And your breast is all cover'd with red.

SOLOMON GRUNDY,
Born on a Monday,
Christened on Tuesday,
Married on Wednesday,
Took ill on Thursday,
Worse on Friday,
Died on Saturday,
Buried on Sunday :
This is the end
Of Solomon Grundy.

JACK SPRAT
Had a cat,
It had but one ear ;
It went to buy butter,
When butter was dear.

ELIZABETH, Elspeth, Betsy,
and Bess,
They all went together to seek
a bird's nest.
They found a bird's nest, with
five eggs in,
They all took one, and left four
in

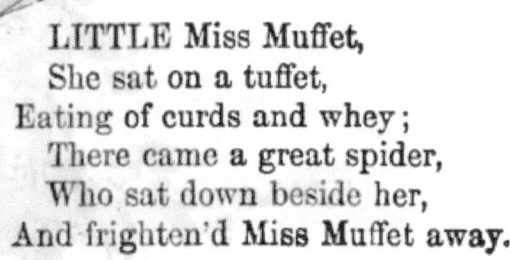

LITTLE Miss Muffet,
She sat on a tuffet,
Eating of curds and whey;
There came a great spider,
Who sat down beside her,
And frighten'd Miss Muffet away.

———

LITTLE Miss, pretty Miss,
Blessings rest upon you;
If I had half-a-crown a day
I'd spend it all upon you.

———

ONE, two, buckle my
  shoe,
Three, four, open the
  door;
Five, six, pick up
  sticks;
Seven, eight, lay them
  straight;

DING dong bell, Pussy's in the well!
  Who put her in?—Little Johnny Green.
Who pulled her out?—Little Johnny Stout.
Oh! what a naughty boy was that,
To drown his poor grand-mammy's cat,
Which never did him any harm,
But killed the mice in his father's barn.

LITTLE Betty Blue
  Lost her holiday shoe,
What can little Betty do?
Give her another,
To match the other,
And then she may walk in two.

HANDY-SPANDY, Jack-a-Dandy,
  Loves plum-cake and sugar-candy.
He bought some at a grocer's shop,
And pleased, away went hop, hop, hop.

THERE was a crooked man, and he went a
    crooked mile,
He found a crooked sixpence against a crook-
    ed stile:
He bought a crooked cat, which caught a
    crooked mouse,
And they all lived together in a little crook-
    ed house.

ONE, two, buckle my shoe;
   Three, four, shut the door;
Five, six, pick up sticks;
Seven, eight, lay them straight;
Nine, ten, a good fat hen;
Eleven, twelve, who will delve?
Thirteen, fourteen, draw the curtain;
Fifteen, sixteen, the maid's in the kitchen;
Seventeen, eighteen, she's a waiting;
Nineteen, twenty, my plate's empty;
Please, mamma, give me some dinner.

SNAIL! snail! come out of your hole,
   Or else I'll beat you as black as a coal.
Snail! snail! put in your head,
Or else I'll beat you till you're dead.

I HAD a little husband, no bigger than my
   thumb,
I put him in a pint pot, and there I bid him
   drum;
I bought him a little handkerchief to wipe
   his little nose,
And a pair of little garters, to tie his little
   hose.

GO to bed, Tom, go to bed, Tom—
   Merry or sober, go to bed, Tom.

THREE blind mice, see how they run!
  They all ran after the farmer's wife,
Who cut off their tails with the carving-
    knife:
Did you ever see such fun in your life?
  Three blind mice.

IF all the seas were one sea,
  What a great sea that would be!
And if all the trees were one tree,
What a great tree that would be!
And if all the axes were one axe,
What a great axe that would be!

MILK-MAN, milk-man, where have you
    been?
In Buttermilk channel up to my chin;
I spilt my milk, and spoilt my clothes,
And got a long icicle hung to my nose.

BLESS you, bless you, bonnie bee:
  Say, when will your wedding be
If it be to-morrow day,
Take your wings and fly away.

HERE we go up, up, up,
  And here we go down, down, downy,
And here we go backwards and forwards,
And here we go round, round, roundy.

THERE was a little guinea pig,
  Who, being little, was not big,
He always walked upon his feet,
And never fasted when he eat.

When from a place he ran away
He never at that place did stay;
And when he ran, as I am told,
He ne'er stood still for young or old.

He often squeaked, and sometimes vi'lent,
And when he squeaked he ne'er was silent;
Though ne'er instructed by a cat,
He knew a mouse was not a rat.

One day, as I am certified,
He took a whim and fairly died;
And, I am told by men of sense,
He never has been living since.

NOSE, nose, jolly red nose,
  And what gave you that jolly · red
    nose?
Nutmegs and cinnamon, spices and cloves,
And they gave me this jolly red nose.

SHOE the horse, and shoe the mare,
  But let the little colt go bare.

www.ingramcontent.com/pod-product-compliance
Lightning Source LLC
Chambersburg PA
CBHW032203010726
47493CB00008BA/2805